This
MOUSE❂WORKS
Classics Collection Storybook

belongs to

_____

DISNEY'S THE 🐚 LITTLE MERMAID

CLASSIC STORYBOOK

MOUSE 🐾 WORKS

Contact us at **www.disneybooks.com** *for more Mouse Works fun!*
Also available in Spanish

© 1989, 1997 Disney Enterprises, Inc.
Adapted by Sheryl Kahn
Illustrated by Atelier Philippe Harchy
Printed in the United States of America
ISBN: 1-57082-727-3
3 5 7 9 10 8 6 4 2

Fathoms below the ocean's surface, in King Triton's kingdom, the sea was bubbling with excitement. All the merfolk and mackerel, sardine and salmon, swordfish and snappers swam as fast as their fins would carry them. No one wanted to miss a single note of the special concert in King Triton's glittering palace.

They gathered in the great hall just as the sea horse announced the arrival of His Royal Highness King Triton. The court composer, Sebastian, tapped his baton and signaled the start of the music.

Six of King Triton's beautiful daughters began to sing as they swirled around the stage. There were Aquata, Andrina, Arista, Attina, Adella, and Alana.

After they had introduced themselves, they turned to present their youngest sister for her musical solo.

All eyes turned to the giant oyster shell center stage. But when it opened, the star of Sebastian's show was missing!

"Ariel!" King Triton bellowed.

But the Little Mermaid didn't hear her father calling her. In fact, she had forgotten about the concert altogether. She had discovered a sunken ship, and couldn't wait to explore it for human treasures to add to her collection.

"Isn't it fantastic?" Ariel exclaimed. "Hurry up, Flounder!"

Ariel and Flounder began to swim through the shadowy ship.

"Have you ever seen anything so wonderful in your entire life?" Ariel gasped, finding a shiny silver fork on the floor.

"Yeah, it's great," Flounder answered nervously. "Now let's get out of here."

"Oh, Flounder," Ariel teased. "Don't be such a guppy."

But no sooner had she spoken than a loud CRUNCH
sounded behind them. "Did you hear something?" Flounder
asked nervously. He turned to find himself staring into the
biggest, meanest, sharpest teeth he had ever seen.

"A shark! Swim!" the little fish cried.

The shark was only inches behind them when Ariel had an idea. She and Flounder squeezed through a hole in an old anchor, and the shark followed. Just as the clever little mermaid had planned, their enemy was too big to fit and got stuck.

"Hah!" bragged Flounder, wiggling his fins in the shark's face. "Take that, you big bully!"

With their treasure safely in hand, Ariel and Flounder swam to the surface to find Scuttle. The silly seagull was a self-proclaimed expert on human things, and he'd surely know what each object was.

"Hmmm," Scuttle murmured, staring at the fork from every angle. "This is a dinglehopper," he said, combing his feathers with it. "Humans use these babies to straighten their hair."

Scuttle had just picked up an old pipe and was explaining how humans played beautiful music on those so-called "snarfblatts" when Ariel suddenly remembered her own music.

"Oh my gosh—the concert!" she cried. "My father's gonna kill me!"

She thanked Scuttle for his help and dove back down beneath the waves, never suspecting that someone was watching her.

"Yes, hurry home, Princess," laughed Ursula. The evil sea witch was hatching a plan.

"As a result of your careless behavior, the entire celebration was ruined," Triton scolded his youngest daughter. "You went up to the surface again, didn't you?"

"I'm sixteen years old. I'm not a child!" Ariel protested.

But it was no use. The King was furious. "As long as you live under my ocean, you'll obey my rules," he said, waving his mighty trident. "You are never to go to the surface again!"

Ariel swam away in tears.

"You don't think I was too hard on her, do you, Sebastian?" Triton sighed. He loved his daughter very much and hated to see her unhappy.

"Of course not," Sebastian said, with a click of his claw. "Teenagers! Give them an inch and they swim all over you! She needs constant supervision."

His Majesty couldn't have agreed more—and appointed Sebastian to keep an eye on the headstrong princess.

Sebastian followed Ariel back to her secret grotto—and he couldn't believe what he saw inside. The sunlight streaming down from the ocean's surface illuminated Ariel's amazing collection of human treasures.

Up above, humans walked and skipped and ran and danced. How she wished she could be part of that world!

The Little Mermaid was daydreaming about having feet instead of fins when a ship sailed over her grotto. She swam to the surface to get a better look.

On board the ship, as part of a birthday celebration for Prince Eric, his faithful guardian, Sir Grimsby, was unveiling an enormous statue of the dashing prince.

As an embarrassed Eric looked at the statue, Ariel looked at Eric. "He's very handsome, isn't he?" she asked Scuttle.

Suddenly a burst of lightning startled the ship's crew to attention. "Hurricane a-comin'!" one of the sailors shouted.

The men began tugging with all their might on the ropes and chains, trying to secure the masts and sails.

But the winds were too strong and the waves too powerful. The ship crashed into the jagged rocks, and Prince Eric was swept into the sea and knocked unconscious.

Ariel dove after the Prince, summoning her strength to pull him to the safety of the nearby shore.

"Is he dead?" she asked Scuttle sadly. He placed his head against Eric's foot and listened hard.

"I can't make out a heartbeat," the seagull replied.

Moved by the handsome prince, Ariel sang to him sweetly.

At the sound of her lovely voice, Eric's eyes fluttered open. Ariel dove back into the sea and watched from a distance as Sir Grimsby helped him back to the palace.

"We're gonna forget this whole thing ever happened," Sebastian insisted.

But Ariel couldn't forget her handsome prince, vowing to return to him someday.

The next day, Ariel was acting very strange. She seemed dreamy and distracted.

"He loves me, he loves me not," she giggled, picking the yellow petals off a sea lily. "He loves me!"

"She's got it bad!" teased her sisters.

"Get your head out of the clouds and back in the water where it belongs!" begged Sebastian. But all Ariel could think about was Eric.

The Sea King was anxious to learn the identity of the lucky merman who had stolen his daughter's heart.

"I know you've been keeping something from me," King Triton said, looking down at the tiny Sebastian.

The crab's teeth chattered nervously. "I tried to stop her!" the crab blurted out. "I told her to stay away from humans."

"Humans?" Triton roared.

Triton burst into Ariel's grotto, furious at his daughter for disobeying him once again.

"If this is the only way to get through to you," he said, raising his mighty trident, "then so be it!" In a rage, he destroyed all the treasures Ariel loved, even the statue of her beloved prince.

Once alone, Ariel looked around at the rubble that had been her beautiful grotto and began to cry.

"Poor child," hissed a voice.

"Poor sweet child," hissed another. Two slimy eels, Flotsam and Jetsam, slithered around her.

"The Sea Witch can help you," they urged her. "She can make all your dreams come true."

Ariel wanted so badly to believe them. Could Ursula, the Sea Witch, really help her and Eric be together forever?

"The only solution to your problem is for you to become human," Ursula cooed. "I live to help poor unfortunate souls like you."

In a puff of pink smoke she showed Ariel what her future could hold—she could have legs! And all it would cost her was...her voice!

As Sebastian and Flounder watched in horror, Ariel signed a contract with Ursula. The wicked sea witch tossed magical ingredients into her bubbling cauldron. She chanted as she stirred the sinister brew.

"Before sunset of your third day on land, you've got to make princie fall in love with you," Ursula cackled. "If he kisses you, you'll remain human. But if not, you'll turn back into a mermaid and belong to me!"

The waters swirled and the ocean floor rumbled. Ariel was tossed and turned by the power of Ursula's evil spell. Her long, beautiful tail split in half and became human legs. No longer a mermaid and unable to breathe under the sea, Ariel was rushed to the surface by Sebastian and Flounder.

On land, Ariel grinned as she wiggled and wriggled her new toes.

"There's something different about you," Scuttle said, studying her. "Don't tell me—it's your hairdo. You've been using the dinglehopper."

"She's got legs!" moaned a disgruntled Sebastian.

"And she's got to make the Prince fall in love with her," Flounder added.

All three friends promised to help her.

What they had to do first was find Eric—which turned out to be easy. Eric's dog, Max, found Ariel first and barked a hello. "You seem very familiar to me," Prince Eric said.

She looked like the girl with the beautiful singing voice who had saved him from drowning. But she couldn't be! If this girl couldn't even speak, how could she sing? He helped her to her feet and back to the palace, secretly wishing that she were the girl with the beautiful voice.

At the castle, Ariel joined the Prince and Sir Grimsby for dinner. Eric couldn't help notice how breathtaking she looked in a shimmering pink gown.

"You look wonderful." He smiled.

"You must be famished!" Grimsby chimed in, as he helped her to a seat at the table.

Sebastian, having barely escaped the clutches of the crazed castle chef, Louis, peeked out from a platter.

"Let's eat before this crab wanders off my plate!" Grimsby announced. But it was too late—Sebastian had already scurried to safety on Ariel's tray.

The Little Mermaid picked up her fork and began combing her hair, just as Scuttle had taught her all humans do with dinglehoppers.

Meanwhile, back under the sea, Triton was worried sick about his youngest daughter.

He had searched every cave and coral reef and left no shell unopened. Ariel was nowhere to be found.

"Let no one sleep," he instructed his royal sea horse messenger, "until she's safe at home."

The next day, Prince Eric gave Ariel a tour of his kingdom. Everything was so different from her world under the sea.

There were people everywhere—laughing, talking, even dancing! It was more wonderful than she had ever imagined!

Eric took her rowing on a peaceful lagoon, surrounded by a curtain of willow trees. It was very romantic—the perfect place to fall in love. Just one thing was missing.

"We got to create the mood," Sebastian said, breaking off a reed to use as a baton. He began to conduct the ducks, turtles, fish, and frogs in a soft love song.

"Did you hear something?" Eric asked. Was it his imagination, or was beautiful music filling the air?

He leaned closer to Ariel and smiled. Their lips were only inches apart.

Flounder and Sebastian watched anxiously—he was going to kiss her! But before the Prince could, the boat mysteriously tipped over!

"That was close—too close," Ursula fumed. "At this rate, he'll kiss her by sunset for sure! It's time I took matters into my own hands."

In a puff of magical smoke, she turned from a hideous octopus into a pretty girl—with Ariel's beautiful voice.

"I'll see him wriggle like a worm on a hook!" she cried.

Eric watched the sun set from the balcony of the palace. Would he ever find the mysterious beauty who had saved him?

"Far better than any dream girl is one right before your eyes," Grimsby advised him.

Eric was about to agree when he heard the sweetest melody floating through the night air. It was Ursula, disguised as Vanessa, with Ariel's beautiful voice coming from the shell around her neck.

Hearing her voice and believing Vanessa must be the one who had saved him from the shipwreck, Eric fell instantly under the wicked spell and decided to marry her.

"The wedding ship departs at sunset," he ordered Grimsby.

"As you wish," Grimsby nodded.

Ariel listened sadly. She had lost her true love forever, and now she would never be able to escape Ursula's evil bargain.

Ursula was delighted—her plan was working perfectly. She was too busy rejoicing to notice Scuttle peeking through a porthole on the wedding ship. He saw her wicked reflection in the mirror, unveiling her true identity.

"The Sea Witch!" he cried. "I gotta tell Ariel!"

"I saw the watch...I mean, the witch...watching the mirror!" the seagull sputtered. He flapped his wings frantically as Ariel, Flounder, and Sebastian struggled to understand him.

"Do you hear what I'm saying?" he tried again. "The Prince is marrying the Sea Witch in disguise!"

Ariel jumped off the dock to rescue Eric. But with her human arms and legs, she could barely stay afloat. Grabbing onto a floating barrel, she let Flounder pull her towards the wedding ship as fast as he could while Sebastian raced off to get Triton.

But there was so little time left—the sun was about to set on the third day, and all would be lost. They had to stop that wedding!

Scuttle tried desperately to interrupt the ceremony.

"Dearly beloved," the minister began, as a flock of bluebirds yanked and pulled Vanessa's hair. All of Ariel's friends—the starfish, the pelicans, even the dolphins—attacked on the seagull's command.

"Get away from me, you slimy..." the witch protested, trying to pry Scuttle away from her.

The magic shell that contained Ariel's voice went flying through the air and landed on the deck, just as Ariel reached the ship. It shattered as the sun descended on the golden horizon.

"Eric?" Ariel spoke at last as her voice returned to her.

"You're the one!" the Prince exclaimed. "It was you all the time."

"Get away from her!" cried Ursula. Eric was about to kiss Ariel—the kiss of true love. But the sun set just seconds before their lips could touch.

"You're too late!" the evil witch grinned triumphantly. In a flash of light, Ariel turned back into a mermaid, and Ursula became her old ugly self once more.

"So long, lover boy," Ursula said, grabbing Ariel and dragging her back into the sea.

"Poor princess!" she cooed. "It's not you I'm after. I've got a much bigger fish to fry."

As she spoke, the Sea King appeared before them, ordering the witch to release his daughter.

"Not a chance, Triton," Ursula laughed, clinging tightly to Ariel's wrist. "She's mine now."

"We made a deal," she laughed, showing him the scroll that Ariel had signed. "Of course," she suggested, "I've always had an eye for a bargain. I might be willing to make an exchange."

With a wave of his trident, Triton signed the document and sealed his fate. He, instead of Ariel, would be Ursula's servant.

Eric couldn't bear to think of his love in the clutches of that evil witch.

"I lost her once. I won't lose her again!" he said, casting a harpoon into Ursula's arm.

Summoning the magic of the King's trident, the enraged Ursula grew and grew to a monstrous size.

"Look out!" Ariel cried to Eric. Ursula's tentacles were everywhere! "You've got to get away from here."

"No," the Prince vowed, hugging her. "I won't leave you."

"Say goodbye to your sweetheart," Ursula chuckled, heading right for Eric. She pointed her trident at the Prince and began to shoot fiery lightning bolts at him.

"Now I am the ruler of all the ocean!" she declared, stirring up a hurricane. "The waves obey my every whim. The ocean bows to my power!"

But the battle wasn't over yet. Eric was hurled back on board a sunken ship that had resurfaced in the commotion. While the ship was crumbling under the power of the tremendous waves, Eric steered the jagged bow of the ship through the blinding wind and rain, straight for Ursula!

The bow pierced right through Ursula's cold heart—and her spell was instantly broken. The Sea Witch disappeared into the water, and the storm died down. Eric escaped to the safety of the shore just as the ship sank slowly to the bottom of the sea.

All the poor unfortunate souls Ursula had tricked into signing her contract, including King Triton, were free at last!

With his crown and trident back in place, Triton gazed at his youngest daughter. "She really does love him, doesn't she?" he said to Sebastian.

Touching his trident to the water, he turned Ariel's tail into human legs once again. As much as he would miss her under the sea, Triton was happy knowing that Ariel had found true love.

Sebastian, Flounder, and all of Ariel's friends gathered to watch her joyous wedding to Prince Eric.

Eric kissed his princess as the humans and merfolk all cheered. At last Ariel was part of the human world she loved so dearly—and she would live there with her beloved prince happily ever after.

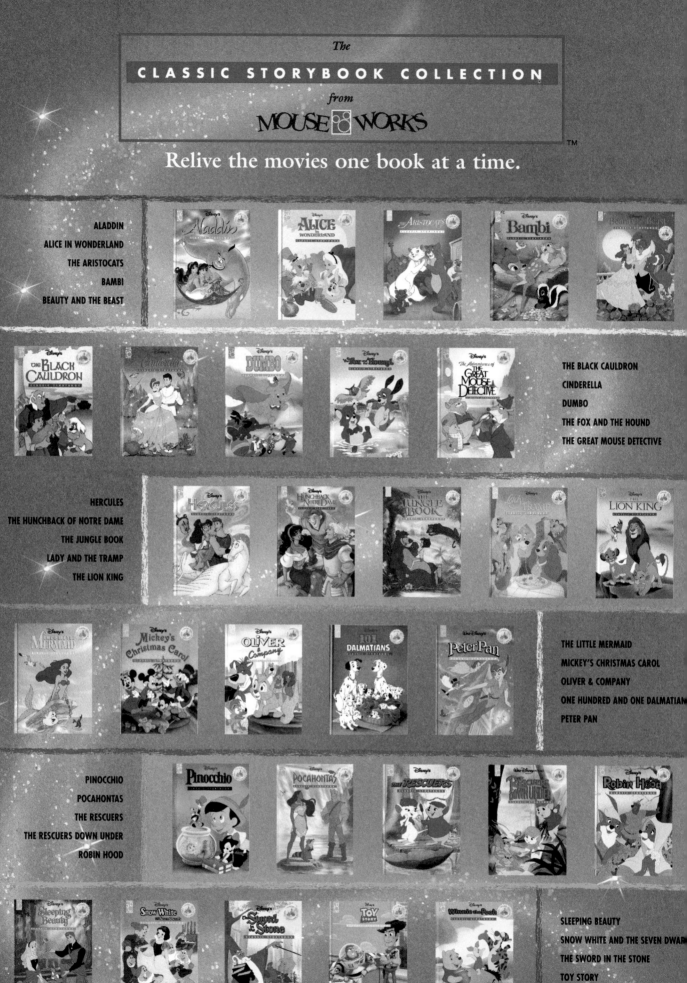

The
CLASSIC STORYBOOK COLLECTION
from
MOUSE WORKS
™

Relive the movies one book at a time.

ALADDIN

ALICE IN WONDERLAND

THE ARISTOCATS

BAMBI

BEAUTY AND THE BEAST

THE BLACK CAULDRON

CINDERELLA

DUMBO

THE FOX AND THE HOUND

THE GREAT MOUSE DETECTIVE

HERCULES

THE HUNCHBACK OF NOTRE DAME

THE JUNGLE BOOK

LADY AND THE TRAMP

THE LION KING

THE LITTLE MERMAID

MICKEY'S CHRISTMAS CAROL

OLIVER & COMPANY

ONE HUNDRED AND ONE DALMATIANS

PETER PAN

PINOCCHIO

POCAHONTAS

THE RESCUERS

THE RESCUERS DOWN UNDER

ROBIN HOOD

SLEEPING BEAUTY

SNOW WHITE AND THE SEVEN DWAR

THE SWORD IN THE STONE

TOY STORY

WINNIE THE POOH